Casey Chief
Kansas City Chiefs

Rip Raider
Los Angeles Raiders

Dolph Dolphin
Miami Dolphins

Pat Patriot
New England Patriots

Jumbo Jet
New York Jets

Stevie Steeler
Pittsburgh Steelers

Charlie Charger
San Diego Chargers

Sandy Seahawk
Seattle Seahawks

Text and illustrations © 1984 Parker Brothers, Division of CPG Products, Corp. All rights reserved.

Library of Congress Cataloging in Publication Data: Hartsell, Lynn. Pitch in and play fair. (The Huddles) SUMMARY: The twenty-eight Huddles who live in Huddlestown with their Coach manage to repair the damage done to their town by a winter storm even after the money they raised for the work is stolen by Charlie Cheater. 1. Children's stories, American.
[1. Behavior—Fiction]   I. Ewers, Joe, ill.   II. Title.   III. Series.
PZ7.H26742He   1984   [E]   84-1150   ISBN 0-910313-75-X
Manufactured in the United States of America   1 2 3 4 5 6 8 9 0   01

Pitch in
and Play Fair

Story by Lynn Hartsell
Pictures by Pat Sustendal

A big storm roared through Huddlestown. The wind was very strong and blew down several big, tall trees. Many of the buildings in Huddlestown had been damaged. The Huddles' clubhouse was hit hardest of all.

The Coach was out of town, so Cowboy Joe gathered a few of the Huddles at the clubhouse to inspect the damage.

"Gee, this place looks awful, doesn't it?" Cowboy Joe asked the other Huddles. "With the Coach returning from his trip soon, it sure would be nice to have the clubhouse and all of Huddlestown back the way it was before the storm."

Packy Packer ran into the clubhouse at that moment. "Did you say the Coach is coming home? Let's have a party! With lots of food!"

"Great idea, Packy!" said Cowboy Joe. "We will have a party — after we've cleaned up Huddlestown. You know the Coach! He always expects everything to be in perfect order. Let's call all the other Huddles to the clubhouse. Reddy Redskin can send out the message. It's Spring Clean-Up time!"

Reddy's smoke signals rose in the air. All the Huddles hurried to the clubhouse. Jumbo Jet zoomed in from his airport hangar. Buddy Bear came out of his cave, and Leo Lion came out of his den. Benny Bengal pounced on them playfully.

Buddy growled, "Leave us alone, Benny! We have no time to fool around. They need us at the clubhouse!"

When everyone was at the clubhouse,
Cowboy Joe said, "Fellow Huddles, the Coach
will be back in four days, and we all want
Huddlestown to look as good as new. Where
should we start?"

"Some big trees blew down — we need to
plant new ones," said Big Red Cardinal.

"A lot of shingles came off our clubhouse roof because of the wind," said Sir Saint.

"That ol' Golden Football statue yonder in the park could tolerate a new coat of gold paint," drawled Freddie Falcon. "Reckon I could do that."

"Of course, we'll each fix up our own house and yard," said Pat Patriot. " 'A stitch in time saves nine,' you know."

Dolph Dolphin looked puzzled. Sometimes Pat used sayings that Dolph just didn't understand.

"These are all good plans," said Cowboy Joe, "but we'll need more money than we've got for shingles and paint and trees. And we only have four days to do everything! How can we earn the extra money?"

"I'll sell plane rides," said Jumbo Jet, who was always eager to fly.

"We can have a fish fry down by the river," said Sandy Seahawk.

Cody Colt and Bucky Bronco both reared up. "How about a Wild West Show — where we can do tricks!" They ran and jumped around the room until Cowboy Joe held up his hand to stop them.

"Fine, but out at my ranch! Not in the clubhouse!"

The Huddles finished their plans to raise money, clean up Huddlestown, and throw a big welcome home party for the Coach. They were very excited.

No one noticed Chuck Cheater sitting on
the clubhouse porch listening. Chuck Cheater
lived with his gang over in Out of Bounds. He
often tried to make the Huddles get into
trouble by being sneaky or dishonest.

"Hah!" said Chuck to himself. "No money,
no clean-up, no party — that will be my plan!"

The fish fry was the very next day. Sandy
caught lots of fish and began to grill them on
the beach near the river. Suddenly he noticed
Chuck Cheater trying to steal away with a
huge platter of fish.

"Hey! Where do you think you're going?" called Sandy.

"Um, I was just, uh, bringing this platter closer to the picnic tables," said Chuck quickly.

"Well, bring it back here right now. And get out of here!" replied Sandy.

Soon everyone arrived, paid their
money, and ate the delicious meal.

Chuck Cheater managed to sneak a dinner
for himself without paying. He tried to talk
Packy into doing the same.

''Go back for seconds,'' Chuck whispered
to Packy. ''No one will notice.''

Packy looked hungrily at the delicious berry pies he had baked. "Gee, I'd love another piece...."

He started to walk towards the pies. But then he changed his mind.

"No, Chuck, it wouldn't be fair to take more without paying more. Besides, I'm getting into shape for football practice."

Later, Sandy Seahawk and Rip Raider were washing dishes. Chuck Cheater came by with a suggestion for them. "Why do you have to work so hard? Let someone else do that," he said. "Let's go to a movie and relax!"

"That sounds like fun," said Rip. He snapped his towel at Sandy.

"We're not working for ourselves,
remember?" asked Sandy. "We're working
for Huddlestown."

Rip agreed. "Right! Chuck, either dry
dishes or dry up!"

Chuck shrugged his shoulders and
walked away.

On the beach, Pat Patriot was loading all the soft–drink cans into an empty trash bag.

"Why are you doing that?" asked Chuck.

"They can be sold," Pat explained. " 'A penny saved is a penny earned,' you know."

"Hah!" said Chuck. "I'd say a penny saved is a penny that could be spent in the gumball machine!"

He tried to grab a bunch of cans and stuff them into his jacket, but Pat ran after him.

"Chuck! Won't you ever learn that 'crime doesn't pay'?" asked Pat. He pulled all the cans out of Chuck's jacket and pushed him away.

"Now run along! I have honest work to do here!"

The next morning, Jumbo Jet hung a big banner on his hangar door.

Jumbo was busy flying all day. Jolly Giant came over from his beanstalk house to sell tickets. Before long, Chuck Cheater came by to talk to Jolly.

"Hey, Big Guy! Think of the candy you could buy for yourself with that ticket money. I'm on my way to the candy store right now. Let's go!"

Jolly Giant thought about
a huge chocolate bar. But then he
thought about the younger Huddles
and how they all looked up to him.
    "Block that thought, Chuck. This
money is for Huddlestown."

Chuck kicked a stone and stomped off. He could never get any of these Huddles to listen to him. They were just too honest for him. And time was running out. The Coach would be back in two more days!

The Wild West Show was at Cowboy Joe's ranch the next day.

First, Casey Chief showed his bow-and-arrow skills. He had on his handsome feather headdress and the beads on his moccasins were polished until they sparkled.

Cowboy Joe amazed the crowd with rope tricks. Then Cody Colt and Bucky Bronco got ready to put on their wild horse show. Cody went out first.

Chuck Cheater was waiting behind the corral to catch Bucky alone for a moment. "Hey, Bucky! Why knock yourself out?" Chuck Cheater asked. "Let's go for a nice long ride in the country instead. What do you say?"

Bucky didn't want to have anything to do with that sort of lazy plan, so he kicked up his heels and rushed out to join Cody. His heels blew up dust, and Chuck got dirty, head to toe.

But Chuck wasn't discouraged. He already had a new plan in mind. If the Huddles wouldn't do what he wanted, he'd make sure that Huddlestown would never be fixed up. That night he tiptoed into the clubhouse. He found the cashbox where Cowboy Joe was keeping all the money the Huddles had made. Chuck Cheater made sure no one was watching. Then he grabbed the money and ran back toward Out of Bounds.

When the Huddles arrived at the clubhouse the next day, they were surprised and angry.

"All our money's been stolen!" cried Freddie Falcon. "Now I won't be able to buy the paint to finish the golden statue. I can't even find what was left of my first can."

"And what about my shingles?" asked Sir Saint.

"And my beautiful trees?" whistled Big Red Cardinal.

Cowboy Joe spoke up. "This is very, very bad news, but we can still work on improving Huddlestown before the Coach returns tomorrow. Each of us can clean up the rubbish that the storm left in our yards. It's better than nothing. When we find the thief and get our money back, we'll do the rest."

The Huddles set to work. They all pitched in and helped each other, and before long Huddlestown looked much better. Yet when he looked around, Sir Saint couldn't help giving a big, sad sigh.

"What's the matter?" asked Leo the Lion.

"We've tried our best," answered Sir Saint, "but the clubhouse roof is still not fixed." Sir Saint looked glum, and before long, many of the other Huddles admitted that they were sad that everything would not be perfect for the Coach's return.

"This won't do," thought Jumbo Jet. "The Coach won't want to see a bunch of sad faces when he returns. I know something that will cheer up everybody." With that, Jumbo Jet roared off into the sky. He was going to write "Welcome Home, Coach" in the sky over Huddlestown. He even had special red, white, and blue smoke to write with.

However, just as Jumbo finished writing "W" he noticed that something was flashing from the ground. Was someone trying to signal him? Did someone need help? Jumbo swooped down to investigate, and he got a big surprise!

There, in the middle of a small clearing in the woods was Chuck Cheater. In front of him was a pile of silver coins. Chuck polished each coin on his shirt, and then held it up to inspect it. When he held the shiny coins out in front of him, they flashed in the bright rays of the sun.

Chuck was so busy with the money that he never heard Jumbo approaching. "I've fooled them at last, those little goodie-goodies," Chuck sneered. "They can't possibly fix up Huddlestown now because I've got all their money!"

When Jumbo heard that, he got angry. "I'll show that Cheater he can't get away with his plan," Jumbo said. He started his engine, zoomed down from the sky, and snatched the money away from Chuck.

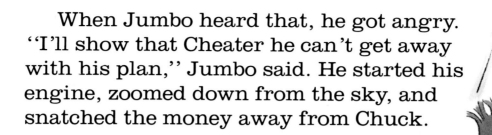

"Hey, come back here!" yelled Chuck. He tried to chase Jumbo, but when he jumped up, he tripped over the can of gold paint that he had hidden from Freddie Falcon.

Angry and covered with paint, Chuck limped back to his home in Out of Bounds. Jumbo wrote a new message in the sky:

"Sorry, Chuck. Cheating Never Pays."

When the Coach returned, he was
delighted with the way Huddlestown looked.
 Sir Saint told the Coach what Jumbo
had done.
 ''I think we should give Jumbo Jet a
cheer,'' said the Coach.

"Let's have a cheer for all of us," said Jumbo modestly.

"We all worked together to make Huddlestown better than ever."

All the Huddles joined in. "Hurrah for fair play! Hurrah for helping! Hurrah for the Huddles!"

NATIONAL FOOTBALL CONFERENCE

Freddie Falcon
Atlanta Falcons

Buddy Bear
Chicago Bears

Cowboy Joe
Dallas Cowboys

Leo Lion
Detroit Lions

Packy Packer
Green Bay Packers

Ramsey Ram
Los Angeles Rams